Too Many Babas

Too Many Babas

Story and pictures by Carolyn Croll

HarperTrophy
A Division of HarperCollins*Publishers*

Too Many Babas
Copyright © 1979, 1994 by Carolyn Croll
Printed in the U.S.A. All rights reserved.
Typography by Al Cetta
❖
Newly Illustrated Edition

Library of Congress Cataloging-in-Publication Data
Croll, Carolyn.
    Too many Babas / story and pictures by Carolyn Croll.
        p.   cm. —(An I can read book)
    Summary: Four peasant ladies discover that too many cooks without a plan can spoil
the broth.
    ISBN 0-06-021383-3. — ISBN 0-06-021384-1 (lib. bdg.)
    ISBN 0-06-444168-7 (pbk.)
    [1. Cookery—Fiction.]   I. Title.   II. Series.
[PZ7.C8767To   1994]   92-18779
[E]—dc20   CIP
                                                                  AC

First Harper Trophy edition, 1994.

For Mom

Baba Edis lived

in a little wooden house

at the edge of town.

One morning when she woke up,

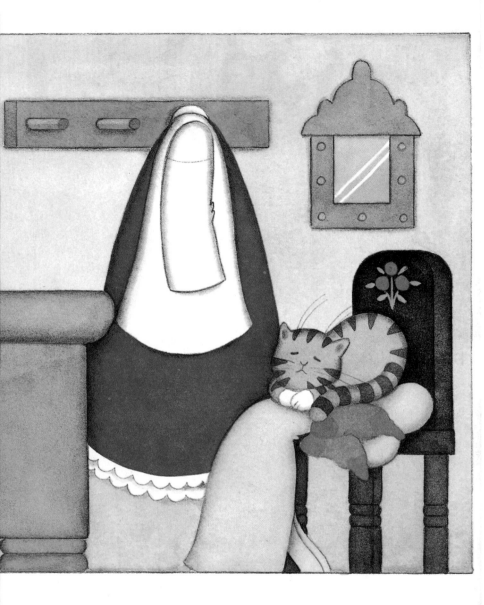

it was very cold.

"This is a good day

to make some soup to warm my bones,"

Baba Edis said as she put on

her woolen dress and stockings.

11

She got out her big, old soup pot,

filled it with water,

and set it on the stove to boil.

"Now let us see what I have,"

said Baba Edis.

There was a bone she had saved

and a cup of beans,

some carrots, celery, cabbage,

and a yellow onion for flavor.

As the soup began to cook,

it filled the air

with a fine aroma.

Baba Basha, who was passing by,

got a whiff of the good smell

and stopped in.

"What is that delicious smell?"

called Baba Basha.

"Just some soup

to warm my bones

on this cold day,"

said Baba Edis.

"You are welcome

to have a bowl

when it is ready."

"I think I will,"

said Baba Basha.

Baba Basha took a taste.

"It needs salt, dear," she said,

and dumped a fistful of salt

into the pot.

Then she tasted it again.

"That's better,"

she said, and sat down.

In a little while

a face appeared at the window.

It was Baba Yetta.

"Come in," called Baba Basha.

"Baba Edis is making soup

to warm her bones

on this cold day,

and if you care to wait

until it is ready,

you can have a bowl yourself."

Baba Edis pulled up another chair.

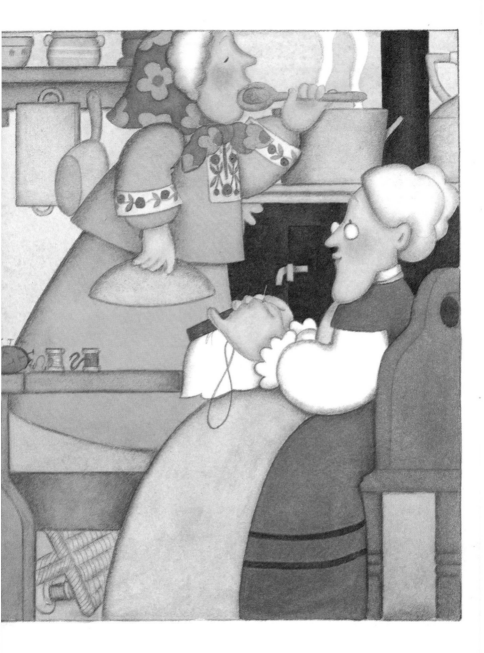

Baba Yetta took a taste.

21

"Hmmmmmm," she said.

"It needs something.

I know!

Pepper!"

Baba Yetta grabbed the pepper grinder

and gave it a good many turns.

"Perfect!" she cried,

and sat down with Baba Basha.

Pretty soon there was

a knock at the door.

"Why, this looks like a party,

and what is that heavenly smell,

Baba Edis?"

It was Baba Molka

on her way home

from the marketplace.

"Please come in and join us," called

Baba Basha and Baba Yetta together.

"Baba Edis is making soup

to warm her bones on this cold day

and has invited us to have some

when it is ready.

There is plenty, and

you are welcome to have some too."

Baba Edis went into her bedroom

to get another chair.

While she was gone,

Baba Molka tasted the soup.

"Hmmmmmm," she said,

and went to her basket

and pulled out a plump garlic bulb.

"A little garlic is just the thing

to finish off this soup," she said,

and plopped in four cloves.

"It will take a little while

for the garlic to do its job,"

she said, and sat down to wait.

Baba Edis got out

the bowls and spoons.

She put a loaf of dark bread

in a basket on the table.

After a while

Baba Basha went to the soup pot

to taste and sniff.

"Hmmmmmm," she said.

"Just a dash more salt

and it will be perfect."

34

"Almost ready?" asked Baba Yetta.

She lifted the lid and took a whiff.

"It doesn't smell spicy enough,"

she said,

and grabbed the pepper grinder.

"Let me give it a stir,"

Baba Molka said,

and took the spoon from Baba Yetta.

"It looks a little thin,"

said Baba Molka.

"Another clove or two of garlic

will give it character."

"I think the soup is ready,"

said Baba Edis.

"I hope you are all hungry."

She ladled the soup into the bowls

and passed them to her guests.

"It looks delicious,"

said Baba Basha.

"It smells delicious,"

said Baba Yetta and Baba Molka.

They all sat down at the table.

Baba Edis said, "I think

too many cooks spoiled my soup.

Now all we have for supper

is bread and tea."

"We are very sorry, Baba Edis,"

said Baba Basha.

"I wish there was a way

to start again," said Baba Yetta.

"Wait a minute!" said Baba Molka.

She reached for her basket.

"I have a cabbage and some potatoes

and beans and carrots.

If we are going to help make soup,

then this time

we need a plan.

Each of us will do one part."

"I'll scrub out the pot
and put water on to boil,"
said Baba Basha.

"I'll wash the vegetables,"

said Baba Yetta.

"And I'll chop them up,"

said Baba Molka.

They all got to work.

Soon the soup was boiling.

Baba Edis was feeling much better now.

She lifted the lid and took a taste.

"Only I will add the salt and

pepper and garlic," she said.

Carefully she measured them out.

Then she tasted the soup again.

When the soup was ready,

Baba Basha, Baba Yetta, Baba Molka,

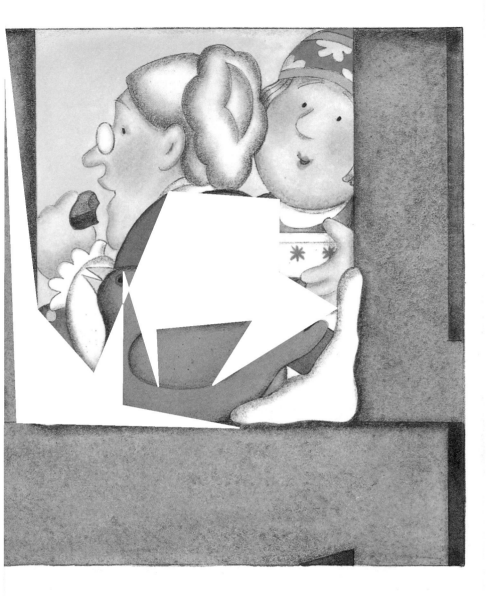

and Baba Edis were so hungry,

they each had two bowls full.

When they were finished,

Baba Basha cleared the table.

Baba Yetta washed the dishes.

Baba Molka dried the dishes.

And Baba Edis put them away.

Then they all said good night.